My First Nursery Rhymes

Illustrations by Mark Davis

**FLAME TREE
PUBLISHING**

Publisher and Creative Director: Nick Wells
Illustration and Layout: Mackerel
Editorial: Sara Robson
Production: Chris Herbert, Claire Walker

ISBN 978-1-84451-401-3

10 9 8 7 6 5 4 3

10 09 08

First published in 2006 by
FLAME TREE PUBLISHING
Crabtree Hall, Crabtree Lane,
Fulham, London SW6 6TY, United Kingdom
www.flametreepublishing.com

© Flame Tree Publishing 2006

Flame Tree Publishing is part of The Foundry Creative Media Co. Ltd.

Printed in Malaysia

A copy of the CIP data for this book is available from the British Library upon request.

Publisher's Note

There are many different versions of these Nursery Rhymes, from many different sources. Different parts of the world, even different parts of the same country have oral traditions with very similar subjects, which were written down over many hundreds of years. The versions in this book represent our best collective view of the rhymes. 'The Owl and The Pussycat' is a nonsense poem written by Edward Lear in 1871. Over the years it has become one of the best-loved children's rhymes.

Contents

Hush-a-bye, Baby

Hush-a-bye, baby,
On the tree top,
When the wind blows
The cradle will rock;
When the bough breaks
The cradle will fall,
And down will come baby,
Cradle, and all.

Jack be Nimble

Jack be nimble,
Jack be quick,
Jack jump over
The candlestick.

Tom, Tom, the Piper's Son

Tom, Tom, the piper's son,
Stole a pig, and away he run;
The pig was eat
And Tom was beat,
And Tom went crying down the street.

The Owl and the Pussycat

The Owl and the Pussycat went to sea in a beautiful pea-green boat;
They took some honey and plenty of money,
Wrapped up in a five pound note.
The Owl looked up at the stars above and sang to a small guitar,
"O lovely Pussy, O Pussy my love,
What a beautiful Pussy you are, you are, you are!
What a beautiful Pussy you are!"

Pussy said to the Owl, "You elegant fowl,
How charmingly sweet you sing!
O let us be married! Too long we have tarried:
But what shall we do for a ring?"
They sailed away, for a year and a day,
To the land where the Bong-tree grows,
And there in a wood a Piggy-wig stood
With a ring at the end of his nose, his nose, his nose,
With a ring at the end of his nose.

"Dear Pig, are you willing to sell, for one shilling, your ring?"
Said the Piggy, "I will."
So they took it away and were married next day
By the Turkey who lived on the hill.
They dined on mince, and slices of quince,
Which they ate with a runcible spoon;
And hand in hand, on the edge of the sand,
They danced by the light of the moon, the moon, the moon,
They danced by the light of the moon.

Incy Wincy Spider

Incy Wincy spider
Climbed up the water spout.
Down came the rain
And washed the spider out.

Out came the sunshine
And dried up all the rain,
So Incy Wincy spider
Climbed up the spout again.

Little Boy Blue

Little Boy Blue, come blow your horn,
The sheep's in the meadow, the cow's in the corn;
But where is the boy who looks after the sheep?
He's under a haycock, fast asleep.
Will you wake him? No, not I,
For if I do, he's sure to cry.

Little Jack Horner

Little Jack Horner
Sat in the corner,
Eating a Christmas pie;
He put in his thumb,
And pulled out a plum,
And said, What a good boy am I!

Goosey, Goosey Gander

Goosey, goosey gander, whither shall I wander?
Upstairs and downstairs and in my lady's chamber.
There I met an old man who would not say his prayers.
I took him by the left leg and threw him down the stairs.

Baa, Baa, Black Sheep

Baa, baa, black sheep,
Have you any wool?
Yes, sir, yes, sir,
Three bags full;
One for the master,
And one for the dame,
And one for the little boy
Who lives down the lane.

Little Miss Muffet

Little Miss Muffet sat on a tuffet,
Eating her curds and whey;
Along came a spider, who sat down beside her
And frightened Miss Muffet away.

It's Raining, It's Pouring

It's raining, it's pouring,
The old man is snoring;
He went to bed
And bumped his head
And he couldn't get up in the morning.
Rain, rain, go away;
Come again another day;
Little Johnny wants to play.

Simple Simon

Simple Simon met a pieman,
    Going to the fair;
Says Simple Simon to the pieman,
    Let me taste your ware.

Says the pieman to Simple Simon,
    Show me first your penny.
Says Simple Simon to the pieman,
    Indeed, I have not any.

Simple Simon went a-fishing,
    For to catch a whale;
All the water he had got
    Was in his mother's pail.

Simple Simon went to look
    If plums grew on a thistle;
He pricked his fingers very much,
    Which made poor Simon whistle.

He went to catch a dicky bird,
	And thought he could not fail,
Because he had a little salt,
	To put upon its tail.

He went for water with a sieve,
	But soon it ran all through;
And now poor Simple Simon
	Bids you all adieu.

Fee! Fie! Foe! Fum!

Fee! Fie! Foe! Fum!
I smell the blood of an Englishman;
Be he alive, or be he dead,
I'll grind his bones to make my bread.

Hickory, Dickory, Dock

Hickory, dickory, dock,
The mouse ran up the clock.
The clock struck one,
The mouse ran down,
Hickory, dickory, dock.

Old Mother Hubbard

Old Mother Hubbard
Went to the cupboard,
To fetch her poor dog a bone;
But when she came there
The cupboard was bare
And so the poor dog had none.

She went to the baker's
To buy him some bread;
But when she came back
The poor dog was dead.

She went to the undertaker's
To buy him a coffin;
But when she came back
The poor dog was laughing.

She took a clean dish
To get him some tripe;
But when she came back
He was smoking a pipe.

She went to the fruiterer's
To buy him some fruit;
But when she came back
He was playing the flute.

She went to the hatter's
To buy him a hat;
But when she came back
He was feeding the cat.

The dame made a curtsy,
The dog made a bow;
The dame said, Your servant.
The dog said, Bow-wow.

Teddy Bear, Teddy Bear

Teddy bear, Teddy bear,
Touch the ground.

Teddy bear, Teddy bear,
Turn around.

Teddy bear, Teddy bear,
Show your shoe.

Teddy bear, Teddy bear,
That will do.

Teddy bear, Teddy bear,
Run upstairs.

Teddy bear, Teddy bear,
Say your prayers.

Teddy bear, Teddy bear,
Blow out the light.

Teddy bear, Teddy bear,
Say good night.

Wee Willie Winkie

Wee Willie Winkie runs through the town,
Upstairs and downstairs in his nightgown,
Rapping at the window,
Crying through the lock,
Are the children all in bed,
For now it's eight o'clock?

Georgie Porgie

Georgie Porgie, pudding and pie,
Kissed the girls and made them cry;
When the boys came out to play,
Georgie Porgie ran away.

The Old Woman who Lived in a Shoe

There was an old woman who lived in a shoe,
She had so many children she didn't know what to do;
She gave them some broth without any bread;
And whipped them all soundly and put them to bed.

Monday's Child

Monday's child is fair of face,

Tuesday's child is full of grace,

Wednesday's child is full of woe,

Thursday's child has far to go,

Friday's child is loving and giving,

Saturday's child works hard for a living,

And the child that is born on the Sabbath day,
Is bonny and blithe, and good and gay.